THE AWAKENING

"All that Lives was Born to Die"

Napoleon Esteban

Books Academy LLC
112 SW H K Dodgen Loop, Temple, Texas 76504
Hotline: (254) 800-1189

Ordering Information:
Quantity sales. Special discounts are available on quantity purchases by corporations, associations, and others. For details, contact the publisher at the address above.

Printed in the United States of America.

ISBN-13:   Softcover   978-1-968807-03-0
              eBook   978-1-968807-05-4

Library of Congress Control Number: 2025911997

INTRODUCTION

Narrated by the Old Zombie

Come closer, child of breath. Yes — you, with the warm skin and fleeting heartbeat. Don't be shy. Sit with me, if only for a moment. My flesh may sag, my eyes long clouded by time, but I have seen what lies ahead…and what lies beneath.

I am the witness. The last echo of your forgotten ancestors. The ancient whisper behind your modern thoughts. And I welcome you to a journey with no clear beginning — and no certain end.

They once said it sweetly: The Butcher, The Baker, The Candlestick Maker. Three simple lives, wrapped in rhyme and reason. But what of the rot behind their routines? What of the hunger beneath their habits?

You see, everything that lives was born to die. But death…oh, death is not final as they told you. Matter changes form, consciousness frays, yet nothing truly disappears. It only shifts, breaks, folds itself into a new skin. A new silence.

So I ask: When does life truly end? When the body falls still? When memory fades? Or is it when we forgot who we ever were?

Within these pages, you will find lives. Real lives. Lives once bursting with ambition, delusion, beauty, and blood. Some ran. Some fought. Some simply faded. But each, in their own way, has arrived here — at the Dead End.

But be warned: this "Dead End" is no simple terminus. It is a mirror. A whisper. A revelation. Peer closely, and you may see a face you recognize.

Could it be the butcher? The baker? Or, perhaps… the one who lit the candle in the dark? Could one of these lives be your?
The Awakening begins now. But endings…endings are never what they seem.

- Napoleon Esteban, The Old Zombie

Birth –
"The Awakening"

Ah, the rupture of silence, the first gasp. Not a cry, but a reckoning. The Shadows part to let you through, slick with promise and veiled in rot.

You enter not with innocence, but with debt. You do not know it, but the world is already carving its name into your bones.

Birth is not the beginning — it is the forgetting of where you came from.

ESTEBAN

The Mirror – "Reflections of Flesh"

You gaze into the mirror and see beauty. But I see scaffolding soon to decay. Your cheekbones, your pout, your glow — currency that will expire. You worship reflections, but mirrors lie. They do not show the worm beneath the skin. Ah, how proud you are now. How fragile you shall be.

ESTEB

Vanity –
"A Crown of Flies"

You wear your ego like a crown, jeweled in likes and leers. But beneath, your scalp weeps. Flies buzz not because they smell the spoil beneath the perfume. You think you are adored, but even the adoration is rotting. Soon, your crown will be a halo of maggots.

ESTEB

The Influencer – "Feeding the Dead"

They follow you like sheep, but sheep too are led to slaughter. Each post is a heartbeat sacrificed. Each click, a brick in the tomb you are building. You don't realize you're embalming yourself in relevance. When the power goes out, who will you be? When the likes stop, who will eat your soul?

ESTEB

Youth –
"The Lie of Forever"

Ah, the stretch of youth, elastic and bright. You run as if time cannot catch you. You laugh, you lust, you leap — but the grave has a stopwatch, not a scythe. Every heartbeat is a drumbeat toward dirt. Enjoy it, little one. The worms are patient.

HAPPY
HALLWEEN

Mother –
"The Womb Remembers"

She gave you breath, blood, and name — but not immunity. Even her love cannot halt the rot. She holds you close, but even warmth fades in the cold hush of eternity. Mother is not forever. Even she will forget your face.

ESTEB

The Child –
"Innocence is a Mask"

You see a child and drink purity. But I see a seed, already swelling with shadow. They giggle in sunlit fields, yet even now, the soil prepares a cradle. No one escapes the curve of decay. Not even the ones who cannot yet spell their name.

ESTE

The Scholar –
"Bones in Books"

He buries himself in pages, believing knowledge grants immunity. But scrolls do not shelter from the shovel. Every theory, every proof, will one day be dust in a forgotten library. Even the clever decay. Even the wise rot.

ESTEB

The Lovers – "Decay in Duet"

Two hearts, beating as one — how poetic. But love is no shield from entropy. They kiss under the stars while the worms write sonnets in their future bed. They whisper forever, but forever is a cruel joke told by the grave. Together, yes. Even in decomposition.

ESTE

The Warrior –
"Iron and Ashes"

He believed his strength would defy it. That muscle and rage could tear through fate. But bones break no matter how bold the stance. The sword rusts. The armor dents. Even the fiercest beast must bow before the quiet. War is loud. Death is louder.

ESTEB

The Preacher –
"Sermons to Silence"

He speaks of heaven while his soul molds. Raises hands to the sky while his feet sink into dust. He fears hell, yet never questions why his god stays silent when the coffin lid shuts. Even prayers smell like flesh to the vultures. Even salvation spoils.

ESTE

The Addict – "Needles and Nightmares

He reaches for fire to feel alive. But every high digs a deeper grave. The shadows love him — he feeds them nightly. He is already half gone, his veins a roadmap of surrender. Some deaths come in slow sips.

ESTEB

The Performer – "Curtain Call"

They dance, they shine, they sparkle beneath the lights. But even stars flicker before the end. Applause is fleeting. The stage is but a polished coffin, And when the curtain falls, they return to the audience of worms — who never blink, never cheer, only consume.

HUARN
ERON
HARVEY
ESTEV

The Prisoner – "Cage of Flesh"

Behind bars, he counts his days. But I tell you, freedom is an illusion. Even the free are imprisoned by breath and blood. His cell is steel. Yours is skin. No one escapes. Not through the gate, not through the good deeds. The grave is only pardon.

ESTEB

The Rebel –
"Ashes of Anger"

She fights the system, claws at the sky. Burns her voice with rage and revolution. But the soil does not take sides. Her bones will lie beside the tyrant's. The fire within her cannot stop the chill beneath. Even rebellion withers. Even defiance decomposes.

ESTE

The Loner –
"Echoes of Silence"

He shuns the crowd, hides from the noise. But death finds him just the same. In the hush, in the hollow, the Shadows are loud. He thinks himself unseen — but the grave has always watched. Solitude does not grant escape. Only a quieter descent.

ESTEB

The Dancer – "Choreography of Dust"

She twirls, floats, defies gravity. She thinks movement makes her immortal. But every step she takes leaves behind a footprint for decay to follow. Grace cannot outpace the rot. Elegance still collapses. Even beauty bruises in the dark.

ESTEV

The Rich Man – "The Weight of Gold"

He built castles from coins, measured his soul in assets. But gold cannot bribe the grave. It glitters, yes — but does not glow in the dark. And when the earth takes him, it will not care for the weight he carried. Only how sweet he takes it to the worms.

ESTEB

The Scientist – "Equations of Emptiness"

He dissected stars, named atoms, mapped the void. But he could never solve the formula of forever. His white coat stains just like any shroud. His legacy? Equations scribbled on the walls of his tomb. Discovery is no shield. Even the universe forgets its own architects.

HALLOWEEN TOWN
ESTE

The Politician – "Power's Corpse"

He stood on podiums and promised eternity. Waved flags stitched with deceit and pride. But power rots faster than flesh. No vote can resurrect. No law can reverse decay. In the end, all rulers lie still — their kingdoms reduced to mulch and memory.

The Artist –
"Canvas of Decay"

She painted souls with color and ache. Created beauty that made mortals weep. But the brush cannot hold back the rot. Her fingers stiffen. Her hues fade. Art may whisper to the future, but even whispers are drowned by the dirt.

ESTEV

Death –
"The Gentleman Caller"

Ah, you know me now. Not the monster you feared, but the silence you ignored. I do not knock. I enter. Not cruel, just inevitable. I wear your face. I hum your name. I am the final kiss you always knew was coming.

ESTEB

Infinity – "Where Shadows Feast"

Beyond the bones, beyond the breath, there is a place where even decay dissolves. No time. No name. No light. Only memory. Only echo. We do not walk there. We become it. And in that final stillness, we are finally whole.

ESTEBA

CONCLUSION

"When you see me again, I hope that you have been the kind of person that you really are now." – Sly Stone

The cycle is not cruel. It is complete. What dies does not vanish. What fades does not fall. It transforms.

So now my reader, turn inward. Gaze not only upon the shadows I have shown you. But the ones that curl within you — quiet, waiting, alive.

Ask yourself: What will remain when your reflection forgets your face? What of you will endure beyond the flesh?

Perhaps the dead do not envy the living. Perhaps they only long to remind them That life, real life, is not how brightly you burn — But how deeply you are felt once the flame is gone.

And so, through our Awakening we go. Not to vanish. But to become something more.

www.ingramcontent.com/pod-product-compliance
Lightning Source LLC
Chambersburg PA
CBHW041143300726
48978CB00016B/1365